Ace in the Hole

SEALed for You

Marissa Dobson

Published by Dobson Ink
Printed in the United States of America
ISBN: 978-1-939978-90-5

Dedication

To all the men and woman in the military who serve our country, and their families.

Contents

Ace Diamond left behind the woman he loved when he joined the Navy SEALs. For years he focused on his career, risking life and limb on missions for his country. Now home on leave, he must face his past and ask himself if leaving her was a mistake.

At seventeen, Gwyneth London gave her heart away only to have it broken. More than a dozen years later, she decides to embrace her single life and have a child on her own. Ready to start over in her hometown, she doesn't expect to see the man who still holds her heart, but when he walks back into her life she's unable to push him away.

Can Gwyneth and Ace claim the life they were supposed to have, or will they let love pass them by?

Chapter One

Ace Diamond tossed his duffle bag at the foot of the steps and admired the peaceful sanctuary he called home. The old Victorian house he was born and raised in was now his. Since purchasing it from his parents after they decided to buy an RV and travel the country, very little had changed. Family photos lined the wide staircase; everything was well used and loved, none of that stuffiness some old houses had. The memories of his childhood played out everywhere he looked.

He'd made it home after months of blood, death, and war that had taken a toll on his body and his spirit. He needed a break, not to mention a week's worth of sleep.

This deployment had been harder than any of the others. Too many of his fellow warriors had been killed. Memories of the bloodshed haunted him every time he closed his eyes. Too many recollections he would have rather left behind. He was a different man than when he left a year ago, and he could no longer look at the world the same way. Everywhere he looked he saw people taking freedom for granted. So many of them didn't even realize that more men and women than he'd care to count gave their lives for those freedoms. This deployment served to remind him just how expensive that freedom was.

Dishes clattered in the kitchen, drawing him from his thoughts and back to the present.

"Wynn?" He made his way toward the large farmhouse kitchen in the rear. Coming around the corner, he expected to find his little sister. Instead, he saw a woman with a short pixie haircut, red hair sticking up every which way, holding a knife in her hand.

"Who are you?" Fear coated her voice.

He looked at the small knife, knowing it would be easy to disarm her if he had to. "Better question is, who are you? After all, you're in my house."

"Ace…" Her eyes widened in surprise. "You're not supposed to be here. Wynn said you wouldn't be back for a couple more weeks."

"Well, I'm here, so why don't you tell me who you are?" He leaned against the wide entryway into the kitchen, crossing his arms over his chest.

"Gwen." With a shaky hand, she set the knife on the counter. "Wynn told me I could stay here until I found a place of my own. I came back for my mother's funeral and couldn't leave. You don't realize how much you miss home until you come back."

"Gwyneth London, it can't be." He took in the woman before him. *Wow!*

"You didn't recognize me at first, so I thought maybe you forgot all about me."

"You look so different." Different was an understatement. Her long blonde hair had been replaced with the spiky, red do, and she had developed curves in all the right places. She was gorgeous. Gathering himself together, he nodded. "I'm sorry about your mom. She was an amazing woman."

"Thank you." She leaned against the counter. "I was making a sandwich. Can I make you one?"

"No thanks, I grabbed something on my way home from the airport, but go ahead." She turned back to the cutting board and cut into the turkey, tomato, and lettuce sandwich. That was when he saw the slight protruding tummy, the beginnings of the curve of pregnancy. Was she?

"You noticed." Sometime while he was lost in his thoughts she turned around, sandwich in one hand, her other hand resting on the curve of her stomach.

"Are you…?"

"Pregnant? Yes."

"Is that the reason you decided to stay?"

"Let's sit, I'll explain while I eat." She moved past him into the dining room, and took a seat at the head of the long dining table. She took a bite out of the sandwich before meeting his gaze. "For years I've been so focused on my career, never sparing time for a personal life, let alone dating or even thinking of children."

"Then how?"

"Two years ago I was in a car accident and was in a coma for weeks. When I woke, I realized there was so much more in life. More that I wanted." She ran her hand over her stomach. "Four months ago I decided I wanted to start a family. So I went to a fertility clinic, and well…you can see the results."

"Why not do it the old-fashioned way?" His eyes widened, appalled that she let a doctor impregnate her instead of doing it the way their parents had.

"To do it that way, you need a man. One-night stands tend to get upset when you use them to have a child without telling them. This seemed a better route."

"But you'll be doing it all on your own. No father to help raise the child."

"I can raise a child myself. My mother practically did it with me, and I turned out just fine. The important part is there's no father to try to take my child away."

She polished off the rest of her sandwich while he sat there trying to figure out what to say to that. Gwen had never been the average woman. No, she had been strong, and full of life. She'd never let a man or anyone tell her what to do.

"I realize you don't agree…"

"What makes you say that?" He didn't like that she found him so easy to read.

"We might have been out of touch for years, but I know you, Ace Le Diamond. I can see the disappointment in your pretty blue eyes. You were raised in a perfect family by both parents. I wasn't so lucky, and my child won't be either, but she'll never lack for anything.

Please don't disrespect my decision just because you don't agree with it."

"Wow." He held up his hands in front of him, warding off her answer. "I said nothing and did nothing to disrespect your decision. I was only thinking back to when we were kids. You always said you wanted a husband, two and a half kids, a dog, and a house with a white picket fence. All these years that I haven't seen you, I just figured you found what you wanted."

He kept to himself that even though Wynn stayed in touch with her, he deliberately lost touch. The attraction between them had always been strong, drawing them together through everything, but when he joined the military, the distance began, only to worsen when he made the SEAL team. She might have been proud of him, but the fear that lingered in her eyes tore at his heart. Distance seemed to be the only way to avoid it.

He had never wanted to cause her any pain, and seeing it there in her eyes he knew the only way to change it was to step back. To let their friendship drift away until she no longer cared about him. It was hard, and over the years he had thought about her, but giving up his career as a SEAL wasn't an option. He was meant for the excitement and the thrill. It was everything he was.

Chapter Two

Gwen couldn't believe Ace was there, sitting beside her. The man who'd stolen her heart. The man who still had it but had no idea. So much time had passed since they'd seen each other, and there he sat looking like not a single day had gone by. Her heart sped, her palms were sweaty, and she felt lightheaded just being near him again. She hated that he had such an effect on her.

She took a sip of the milk she had brought in with her sandwich. "I'll call my realtor and see if she can find me a short term apartment to rent while I'm house searching. If not, I can get a hotel room."

"There's no reason to do that. My mission ended early but I've been reassigned to a training mission. I leave in three days, so you might as well stay put."

"I don't want to be in your way." Nor was she sure she wanted to be alone with him for three days when she couldn't seem to get control of her emotions now.

"You won't be, but if it becomes an issue for either of us I can bunk at Wynn's. I'm assuming you took over the master bedroom, so I'll stay in the guest room."

"Guest room? You mean the storage area." She teased, giving her something to say besides the fact that she took his bedroom to be close to him. It sounded stupid, especially since she hadn't seen him in years, but being in his house brought back all the old feelings she buried deep within her.

"When I bought the house from Mom and Dad, I was leaving for a deployment. I barely had time to get my stuff from my condo and bring it over here. Since then, it's just kind of piled up in that room. I keep hoping one day, between deployments, I'll be able to deal with it, make room for it or just get rid of it, but it never happens."

"Wynn said you're never here, she can't figure out why you wanted this place anyway."

"It's home. It might sound cheesy but if ever the day comes when I can have a family of my own, I want them here. I want the pictures that line the staircase to be of my children and family, to have them enjoy the treehouse my father and I built when I was a kid. Silly, right?"

"No." She shook her head, wishing she could do the same with her child. For that, she'd have to have a place she considered home. Instead, she was going to find a cute little house on the edge of town, with a little land that her daughter could play in.

"It doesn't matter how long I'm gone, when I walk through the front door I feel like I'm at home. I never had that with my condo. Plus, I couldn't picture someone else living in this house. It's the

Diamond household, and since Wynn wasn't going to move out of her beach condo, I bought it."

The Diamond household.

Oh, she knew what that meant. It was so much more than just a name. They'd had some amazing parties in this house, and had a tendency to do it Vegas style. Not hard to believe since Mrs. Diamond had named her kids for their poker party days. The Diamonds weren't gamblers, they preferred playing for favors or candy. Nothing illegal, but they played it like it was all or nothing. No one who knew them was surprised when she named the children Ace, Lucky, and Wynn.

The silence ticked by until he finally spoke. "Moving back here, what about your career?"

"I'm a virtual legal researcher, so it can be done anywhere there's internet. Plus, the company I work for has a second branch in downtown Virginia Beach, so if I ever need to go into the office, there's one close."

"Where were you before?"

"Nashville, Tennessee, that's where the main branch of Madison and Strine is. They hired me fresh out of college."

"What did they have to say about…your pregnancy?"

"They only know I'm pregnant, not how." She ran her hand over the curve of her stomach. "I paid for everything off the books, didn't use my insurance for any of it. Not because I'm embarrassed by my choice, but because it was no one's business."

"Instead your employer thinks you've slept around."

She shot to her feet. "How dare you!"

"I apologize, that was out of line." Remorse was clear on his face.

"Damn right it was. You have no right to judge me."

"Gwen, I'm sorry, I just wasn't thinking. This all came as a shock. I never expected you to go about it the way you have."

"I've changed from the little girl you used to know." She grabbed the plate and glass from the table. "There's a lot that's happened over the years that would shock you. Maybe if you would have stayed in touch, you'd know." She stormed off into the kitchen before the tears came.

One of the things she hated most about being pregnant was the tears. She hated being so emotionally uncertain. She could cry at any moment, and the next she'd be laughing as if nothing happened. *Hormones.*

The soles of his boots echoed on the hardwood floor as he followed her. "Listen, Gwen, I am really sorry. I know it doesn't change anything, but I am."

"You're right, it doesn't. Sorry doesn't fix anything; it doesn't mend hurt feelings." She placed the dishes in the dishwasher and started cleaning up the counter without looking at him.

He leaned against the island behind her, and kept his words low as if he wasn't sure she should hear him. "All these years I hoped you had found a wonderful man and had that perfect family you always wanted."

Pain shot through her heart. "You never bothered to ask Wynn what happened? Every time we talked I made sure to ask about you."

"No." It came out in a low whisper. She wasn't sure he'd spoken until she turned around and saw him shaking his head. "I didn't…I had hoped if I left things be, then you would be able to find someone to give you everything you deserved. We both know I wasn't the one to give you what you wanted."

"You *chose* not to be that person, without even giving me a say in it." She didn't bother to wipe away the tears that were freely falling down her cheeks. "What did you think would happen? That I'd just forget about you, the time we shared together, and find someone new? Do you really think I'm that much of a bitch?"

"I never said that. Damn it, Gwen, I did what I thought was right." He slapped his hand on the counter.

"Here I thought I always had a say in what was right for me." She threw the dishrag in the sink. "Just forget it."

Chapter Three

Shocked and unable to believe how quickly things had gotten out of hand, Ace just stood there watching Gwen stalk from the kitchen. She was upset, tears streaming down her face, and he wasn't sure how to make anything better. When he put distance between them, he did it for her. It hadn't been easy for him, but neither was seeing her again.

He wanted to believe that all those years ago, he had made the right decision, that he wasn't the reason she was single and pregnant now, but for the first time he had some serious doubt. Seeing her there in his family home brought back all the memories, bringing to life all the feelings he had for her.

Every part of him itched to go after her, to comfort her. Instead, he kept himself rooted to the spot. Feeling her in his arms would be the end of him. He'd never be able to stuff his emotions and hide them away again. Before he realized it, he was halfway across the open space, nearing the steps.

"Get it together, Diamond." With one last glare at the steps, he forced himself to turn away from them. He'd get himself under control, and then go upstairs and get some rest.

In three days, he'd be leaving again. He couldn't forget his life revolved around training and missions, there was nothing left over for a committed relationship. Gwen needed a man who would be there, and now she needed a father for her child. He couldn't be that, and thinking otherwise wasn't fair to her.

His cell phone rang, pulling him back from the brink of his dangerous thoughts. He snatched it from the table and checked the caller ID.

Rebel. What trouble is he getting into now?

Luke "Rebel" Rodríguez wasn't that much younger then Ace, but he partied like he was still twenty-one. Wherever he went he managed to find trouble. It didn't matter where he was or what he was doing, trouble followed him around like a shadow.

He slid his finger across the screen, and brought it to his ear. "I thought you'd be catching up on your sleep so you could get crazy tonight."

"I'm about to do just that. I'm surprised you're not already asleep. Diamond, with your old age, you need your rest. The guys and I are going out tonight, hitting this new club downtown. You coming?"

"No man, I already promised Wynn I'd stop over tonight." The excuse slipped out before he could stop himself. They had barely been off duty for a couple of hours and already Rebel was looking for fun. This time Ace wanted nothing to do with it. He wanted to stay home and maybe find a way to make up his blunder to Gwen.

"Come on, old man. You can do that early, then meet us for drinks."

"Next time, you have my word. Have a good time."

"Damn man, you and Boom are getting too old for your own good. Successful missions should be celebrated, you never know when the next one might be our last."

Wasn't that the truth, but not tonight.

"Boom?" He and Jared "Boom" Taylor were in the same SEAL class, going through the torture of training together. Sticking together, they'd somehow made it through when most of their class dropped out.

"Yeah, he's staying home tonight too. Something about a list of shit to do before we leave again."

He didn't like the fact that the boys were going out without him or Boom; they were the ones that kept the younger men in line and out of jail. "What's the name of the club?"

"Pulse. It's off Mediterranean Avenue, just past the Japanese restaurant. You can't miss the signs. Does that mean you're coming then?"

"I might stop by." He left it open, so if he didn't feel like going, no one would be watching out for him.

"See you there." Excitement poured from Rebel's voice.

"Maybe," he reminded him before ending the call.

Just what I want to do, go out to a loud club. Don't the boys believe in resting at all?

With a shower calling to him, he slid the phone into his pocket, grabbed his sea bag and headed upstairs. Shower, some sleep, and then hopefully he'd have an idea how to fix the tension between Gwen and him without getting too close to her.

Gwen curled up on the king size bed. The tears had finally begun to subside when the shower kicked on in the hall bathroom. She had debated leaving. At this time of year, she could find a hotel without a problem, but something kept her there. Seeing Ace brought everything back with a vengeance. It broke her heart to hear the only man she ever loved stand there and criticize her choices.

It took a near fatal car accident to make her realize she couldn't keep waiting for him. She had to move on with her life. She fell in love with Ace in high school and never got over it. Even the few short-term boyfriends she'd had since then could never compare to him.

She'd once believed they would spend their lives together, though she hadn't been comfortable with the idea of being a military wife. That was where his ambition was, and she had accepted that. Then he just went off to boot camp and never looked back.

She didn't understand how he could just leave her without explaining it to her. All she received was a Dear Jane letter. She had hoped to be able to talk some sense into him, to get him to see reason, but every letter she wrote went unanswered. Finally, she decided to wait until he came back, but each time he had a break in his training, he made an excuse. By the time he finished his training and joined SEAL team two, she had moved to Tennessee and was busy with her own career. Too much time had passed for her to seek him out; there was no logic left, only pain.

Sliding her hand along the curve of her stomach, her thoughts turned to her unborn daughter, and she tried to convince herself everything had worked out fine. Maybe not the way she wanted them to, but that didn't matter anymore. Now she had to focus on making a life for her and her daughter, and the first step was to find a new place to live.

Chapter Four

Two houses down, Gwen and her realtor stood outside a condo building. The building was two blocks from the beach and just down the road from Wynn's. It was at the top end of her budget, but still within reach if it didn't need a lot of work.

"This condo has two bedrooms, two baths, and the open floor plan you asked for. It also has a den you could use as your office." Trudy read off the house details while Gwen looked over the outside.

"What floor?"

"The eighth floor. There's a large balcony with nice views, as well as a play set on the other side of the building for the children. There's an indoor pool and fitness area, a large area on the first floor that can be used for birthday parties, events, pretty much anything a tenant needs. Shall we go inside?"

She nodded and followed her realtor to the door. The additional amenities the condo provided were appealing. So far, the only thing that wasn't was the additional housing fees associated with it.

"I know it wasn't entirely what you were looking for, but I think it might work better for you. The building next door has a daycare that a lot of the families who live here use. The beach and almost everything you need is all within walking distance."

Another couple of positives for the condo that she added to her mental list. At this point, she didn't plan to use daycare. Her hours were flexible enough that it wasn't needed. She could always hire a daytime nanny if she needed someone to watch her daughter while she worked. That would allow her daughter to be home with her instead of in a daycare.

Inside, the creamy white marble tile and warm gold walls gave the place a touch of class. A small coffee area sat cattycorner to the door, with the television overhead tuned into one of the daytime soaps. It felt welcoming, almost as if it wasn't a lobby.

"There is security detail 'round the clock, they make sure there is fresh coffee out here at all times," Trudy explained, winking.

"Security?"

"There's nothing to worry about. There are never any issues, they're here as a precaution. So close to the beach, many of the condo owners are not year-round residents, so the condo board decided it would put many of the owners at ease to have the security on site." Trudy pushed the up button in front of the bank of elevators.

The elevator doors opened and Lucky was standing there, Ace's younger brother. "Gwen? I can't believe it! That's you, isn't it?"

"Oh, Lucky, how nice it is to see you." She stepped into the elevator and wrapped her arms around him. "It's been too long."

ball with the boys and to scare off any dates the daughters might have."

"As noble as the thought was, it should have been *our* decision to make, not yours. I don't think it worked out as you wanted it to anyway." She smirked and laid her hand on the top curve of her stomach.

"Maybe not how I had hoped, but what matters is your happiness." He laid his hand over hers on her stomach. "I know how important children were for you."

"If you're seeking my forgiveness, you have it. I made peace with what happened a while ago."

"Forgiveness is great in its own way, but that's not the reason I'm telling you this. It should have been done a long time ago. I should have told you so you understood why. It had nothing to do with anything you did…or because I didn't love you."

Even as he sat before her, he realized he'd loved her then, and he still loved her. That was what made the situation so much more difficult.

Chapter Six

Curled up in front of the fire with a warm blanket, Gwen laid the book on her lap and let her head rest against the back of the sofa. It was a perfect evening. One she had been having almost every night this week. She couldn't resist curling up with a good book in front of the fire, but tonight was different. She couldn't get her thoughts away from Ace.

Even after having her heartbroken by him, she couldn't get him out of her system. She longed to feel his touch. If only they could pick up where they left off. She dragged her hand through her spiky hair and enjoyed the moment. At least the tension that had been there before was gone.

"Why didn't you tell me you bumped into Lucky?"

His words pulled her from her thoughts. "You sidetracked me when I got in and I forgot. He wanted me to pass on the invitation to his place for dinner. You're supposed to text him your response tonight so he knows."

He held up his cell phone. "I know. He just texted me. He suggested I send you to bed without supper, like Mom always threatened, for not telling me."

"Your mom would have never done that."

"No, but she threatened. So, little lady, shall I force you to bed?"

Her hormones were playing with her heart and soul; if she wasn't careful they'd lead her to dangerous waters. "Try me, if you're man enough."

He tossed his phone aside and stalked toward her. "That sounds like a challenge. One I think I should take you up on." Taking hold of her hand, he pulled her up out of the chair, the blanket sliding down her legs to land in a pile at their feet.

"Ace."

"Yes?" He scooped her into his arms.

"Put me down." Instead of doing what she asked, he pretended to drop her, forcing her to squeal. "Ace Le Diamond, I demand you put me down." She tried to fill her voice with authority but it was hard with his cologne filling each breath.

"You know I won't drop you."

"What are you doing?" She resisted the urge to rest her head against his strong chest. "You're not putting me to bed."

"It's been so long and I've missed you. Is it wrong that I just want to feel you against me?" He sank down onto the sofa, taking her with him. "If it is, I don't want to be right. I just want to hold you. Is that too much to ask?"

"No, it's not." She let herself relax in his embrace, her head resting on the curve of his shoulder. She began to wonder what it might have been like if they'd never drifted apart. Maybe they'd be sharing this same moment as a married couple, the child she was expecting his. Fantasies, yes—but it was what she wanted.

His lips brushed against the top of her forehead. "This is nice."

She leaned away and looked into his eyes, hoping to find the answer she needed. She needed to know if she was just another girl to fill the time before he left again, or if there were feelings within him that burned for her.

"I can't do this."

"What?"

"I can't…" She took a deep breath and pushed away the tears. "Ace, I never stopped loving you. All these years I waited for you, hoping one day you'd see reason and come back. When I woke up from the coma, you were the one person I wanted at my bedside, but then I realized it was never going to happen. Instead of giving my heart away to another, I buried it deep within me and decided to do this alone."

She ran her hand over her stomach, knowing she had to do this not only for herself but for her daughter. They couldn't live in the same town together if he broke her heart again. "I can't do this because I can't risk you going off on your next training or mission or whatever the hell you want to call it and deciding what's best for me."

"Wait." With one arm, he held tight as she tried to wiggle out of his embrace. He reached behind him, grabbing his wallet. "Every day

I've carried this with me." He pulled out a creamy white ribbon with pink stitches along the edges. "It's my lucky charm, always keeping me safe, no matter how dangerous things get. I never stopped loving you."

Seeing that ribbon sent her memories racing back to that night, only hours before he shipped off to boot camp. They'd sat on the beach, watching the waves crash onto the shore, his arm around her. Back then, it wasn't supposed to be goodbye, only a short time apart until his training was over. Even knowing he was supposed to come back and they'd be together again, her heart broke.

He untied her hair from the ribbon, letting it down to blow in the wind, and whispered sweet promises in her ear. Promising they'd be together forever, he tied the ribbon around his wrist and pushed her gently back onto the blanket, kissing her.

"Do you remember what happened that night?"

His words pulled her back from the memories. It was the first and only time they made love. She lost her virginity to a man she thought she'd spend the rest of her life with. One who ended up leaving without so much as an explanation.

"I remember." As much as it warmed her heart to know he had kept that with him, it didn't change things. "I remember what happened that night, but what is more important is what happened after…"

"Gwen." He slid his hand down her thigh. "I made a mistake, but there's no reason we should suffer from my stupidity any longer. We deserve a second chance."

"Ace." She cupped his cheek, feeling the smooth skin under her fingertips, and gazed into his forest green eyes. "I can't…it's too much for me. I'm sorry, but I can't risk you breaking my heart again when you leave. You said it yourself, you're only home for three days, then you'll leave again and the same thing will happen."

Unable to sit there any longer, she slipped from his embrace, putting distance between them. She needed to be alone, so she grabbed her coat from the hall closet before heading out the front door.

It might not have been the smartest move, but it preserved her heart. Forcing away the tears, she thrust her hands into her pockets and tried to steady her breathing. Following her urges could land her back in the same position she'd been in all those years ago. There was no way she'd let that happen again.

Chapter Seven

Ace stood there stunned beyond belief as he watched Gwen storm out of the house. It was unlike her not to face a problem head on. Unwilling to screw this up again, he slipped his shoes on and decided to follow her. He understood where she was coming from, but damn he wanted her. Having her body pressed against his made everything come back. His job was dangerous, and the commitment she needed was one he wasn't sure he'd be able to give…no matter how much he wanted to. Even so, he had to make it clear how much he cared.

Outside, he looked both directions but couldn't see her anywhere. How she had managed to disappear when he was only minutes behind her, he had no idea. Going with his gut he headed to the park, imagining it would give her a place to sit and think. Not wanting to lose her, he took off in a steady jog, scanning each side street as he passed.

Three blocks later, he entered a picturesque neighborhood, fall leaves scattered on the ground. It was quiet, deserted at that time of night. Headlights illuminated a few small brick houses, then the small car motored off. Gwen sat just down the path on one of the benches that overlooked the playground area, her hand rubbing small circles over her stomach. The dim light caught the glistening tears running down her face.

Damn it, this is why I left. I never wanted to cause her pain, but here I am screwing up her life again.

He needed to make it right. If she chose not to pursue things between them, he'd have to respect that, but until he said what he needed to, he wouldn't back down. If things were going to work between them, she had to be able to accept everything as it was—his job and their past.

"Gwen…" He sat down on the bench next to her and kept his gaze on the playground before him. She barely acknowledged him. "Years ago, I screwed up. I should have been upfront and discussed things with you. Instead, I made the decision without even consulting you. It was wrong of me, but I thought I was doing what was best for you."

"What's done is done, none of it matters now." Her voice broke.

"It does." He turned and laid a hand over hers. "I don't deserve it, but I believe we were given this second chance for a reason."

"I have a child to think about," she snapped. "I wouldn't just be risking myself, but my daughter. I can't…"

"We have months before she's born, let's take time to explore things between us." He laced his fingers through hers. "I can see the look in your eyes. There's still something between us, and it's not just hard feelings. Tell me you don't still love me, and I'll let it go."

"I…" She shook her head, then wiped her nose.

"See, I knew you couldn't, because I can't deny it either." He scooted closer to her on the bench, closing that last remaining distance.

"Maybe love isn't enough." She wouldn't look at him as she said it, giving him the impression she didn't believe it.

"Let me prove to you that it is." They sat there in silence for what seemed like ages, but finally he couldn't wait any longer. "I understand it doesn't seem like enough. Maybe what I can give you isn't what you want, but I do love you. Being a SEAL is who I am. If I thought anyone would understand, it would be you."

"I've never asked you to give it up. It's what you've always wanted, and now you have it. Was it worth what you lost?"

"Is it wrong to want everything?" He turned on the bench so that he could look at her. "When I left, you were only seventeen. I had planned to complete my training and come back for you. To marry you and give you everything you ever wanted. I wanted to wait until I knew I could do it, because if I failed…I didn't know what I'd do."

"I knew you wouldn't fail, it's not who you are." For the first time she met his gaze, telling him she had more faith in him than anyone else. "You worked so hard to prepare yourself before you left. I never doubted you."

"I failed in the one part that mattered most. I failed you, Gwen." As the tears streamed down her face, he pulled her against his chest, holding her as if she was all he had left. "No excuse changes that."

He let her tears subside before adding, "Let me prove I'm worthy of you. This time I won't make the same mistake."

With her arm around his waist, she kept her head pressed against his chest. "I don't think the timing is right. I'm pregnant." There wasn't regret in her voice but maybe disappointment, as if she thought they'd miss their second chance at love.

"On the contrary, I think it's the perfect time. Give *us* a chance. There's no other way to prove to you that it won't happen again, unless you give us a chance." He ran his hand along the curve of her back, hoping she wouldn't turn away from him.

"You'll leave and things will end again. I can't take that pain." Her voice broke. She pulled back from his embrace, biting hard on her bottom lip. "I don't care what people say. It *isn't* better to have loved and lost."

"There's a reason we were brought back together, that my mission ended early and you were here." He gazed down at her and hated that the tears were because of him. "Let's take it slow. Seventy-two hours isn't enough time for me to convince you, but when I come back from this training, I should be home for a while, unless a mission comes up. Then you'll know I'm not going to make the same mistake and I'll have time to properly show you what you mean to me."

"Slow, okay?" The tears were gone now, faint lines marking her face where they fell.

He nodded and kissed her forehead. "Whatever pace you want is fine with me. Come, let's go home, sit by the fire and warm up. On the way, you can tell me about your home search today. Lucky mentioned you were looking at a condo in his building." He kept his arm around her waist and led her back the way they had come.

"My realtor, Trudy, showed me a few places," she mumbled, her head against his chest. "One of them was the condo next to Lucky's. I thought I wanted a house, but this place had everything I wanted and more. The views are good, considering it's not right on the beach, but the roof top deck is amazing. If I want it, I'll have to make an offer soon."

"Lucky says the place is quiet most of the time. I think he's the only bachelor living there. Don't let his bitching about that confuse you, he loves it. Everyone takes such good care of him. I don't think he's ever had to cook a meal. Someone is always bringing him something, checking on his place while he's deployed. He's got it too good there, it's almost like living with Mom, but with more freedom."

"Your mom taught both of you how to cook. Why's he letting others do so much for him?"

"Cooking for one loses its appeal quickly. He repays the favor either with his delicious desserts, or by doing something else for them." He chuckled to himself at the life his little brother was living. Carefree and fun was the best way to describe it.

"I remember those desserts he used to make. If he still has that same sweet tooth, I'm surprised he's in such good shape. I don't think he has an ounce of fat on him."

"It's his training. He might have it easier than me, but he still works off those sweets." He tried to laugh it off, knowing that Lucky was in just as much danger as he was on some missions. He might be deployed less frequently, but the Marines were still the first ones to a battle.

Not wanting to remind her just how dangerous his career was, he teased his fingers along the curve of her shoulder and changed the subject. "Maybe you should hold off putting an offer on a house."

"What?" She tipped her head back to look up at him.

"There's no reason you can't stay here." As they stood outside of his house, he kept his fingers moving over her shoulder, hiding his worry that she'd reject the idea. "I can deal with the shit in the guest room and it could be set up as a nursery. More importantly it will keep you close."

"That's too quick." She tensed under his touch. "Plus I have stuff in storage waiting for me to find a place."

"Just hold off until I'm back from this training."

"Why is it so important to you?"

"In my career, time is limited. I want to spend every opportunity I can with you, to show you what you mean to me." When she said nothing, he added, "The training will only be seven days. That's nothing when you're thinking about the purchase of a house."

"Okay. Unless the perfect place comes on the market, I'll hold off putting a bid in."

"Thank you." A ding from the cell phone in his pocket reminded him the guys were probably wondering where he was. He didn't care, he had everything he wanted right here. Tomorrow he'd smooth things over with the guys, but for tonight he was going to enjoy every moment he could with Gwen in his arms.

Keeping his arm around her body, he held her close and tried not to think what the morning would bring for them. Exhaustion ate at every part of him, but that wasn't uncommon for him. Instead of sleeping he wanted the moment to last, as if he was worried tomorrow he'd wake up and it would all be a dream.

Chapter Eight

There was a certain comfort to sitting across from her while she worked, as Ace went through the mail that had piled up while he was away. It was as if it was always meant to be this way—he and Gwen, together.

The ringing of the doorbell distracted him. "I'll get it." He rose from the table. *Then I'll kill whoever is ruining my peaceful moment.*

Ready to decapitate whoever was at the door, he pulled it open. Boom stood on the porch leaning against the pillar. They might have been best friends, but he wasn't completely thrilled to see him. It wasn't just the fact that he interrupted a quiet day with Gwen. Wherever he went, things had a tendency to erupt. He was the team's demolitions expert, but when he arrived things had a tendency to explode around him, landmines and everything else that got in his way, and he walked away unharmed every time.

"What happened to you last night?" Boom narrowed his eyes, his big arms crossed over his barrel chest.

Ace stepped onto the porch and closed the door behind him; the last thing he wanted was Boom exploding the already delicate situation with Gwen. "I stayed in, not that you were going to be there anyway. Why are you up before sunset?"

"The guys called, seems Rebel got himself into it with a drunk in the parking lot. Our little medic almost ended up in jail."

"Why can't they go out and not cause any problems?" Ace mumbled.

"You remember what it was like."

"Yeah, I remember, but we got the shit kicked out of us for it." He didn't want to think about all the times they had to put in an extra training session because they blew off a little too much steam for their commanding officer to overlook. "Does Mac know?"

"Oh yeah. He'll ride Rebel hard when we head off for our refresher."

Refresher? What a nice way of putting this shitty training mission. The higher ups ordered Mac and the other COs to conduct an advanced close quarter combat training, after one of the other SEAL teams got jammed up.

"Ace?" He turned to see Gwen peeking out the door. He hadn't even heard it open. "Wynn's on the phone for you."

"Could you tell her I'll call her back?"

"So that's why you didn't go out last night." Boom smirked when Gwen closed the door. "Who's she?"

"Gwen… Gwyneth London. You remember her from school?"

"No way…" Boom stepped closer to the window, trying to peer in. "She looks so different…and pregnant. What's she doing here?"

"It's a long story, but she's going to be staying here for a bit." Ace didn't want to get into all the details with Boom, especially since he didn't know where he stood with Gwen.

"Oh man." Boom returned to his spot against the pillar. "Please tell me you aren't getting involved with her."

"What's that supposed to mean?"

"Dude, she's pregnant." Boom stated it as if that made some kind of difference.

"I can see that. How do you know it's not my child?" The words escaped Ace's lips before he had time to think about it, and he realized he wished it was true.

"You mean besides the fact we've been gone over six months? You couldn't hold something like this from me. We've been best friends since third grade. I know you, and you don't need to get involved with an instant family. Man, you don't have to go around saving everyone. Think of yourself for a minute and not about the damsel in distress. Have you stopped to think that maybe she came to you because she knew you'd help her?"

"Boom…" Ace took a deep breath and kept his hands to himself instead of wrapping them around his friend's neck. "We've been friends for a long time, which is why I'm going to let you leave now without killing you."

"You're not thinking…"

"No man, *you're* not thinking. You know nothing about the situation." Ace gritted his teeth, angry that his friend thought so little of Gwen.

"Then tell me. Tell me I'm wrong, and I won't say another word."

"You're wrong. Her mother passed away while we were deployed and she's moving back into town. Wynn told her she could stay here while she was house searching since it was empty. Now I've got to call Wynn, and get ready for a family obligation."

Boom pushed off the pillar and strolled down the steps before turning back to Ace. "If you think that's all there is to it, you're fooling yourself. I saw how she looked at you. There's love in her eyes…stronger than when we were teenagers. Don't think you'll be able to walk away from her like you did before. This time there'll be a child involved and you're too kindhearted for that."

"I'm not walking away this time." Ace growled, his voice edged with anger.

"That proves my point. You think you can save her."

Ace shook his head. "It's not about saving anyone. I love her."

"What about your career? You said before it wasn't fair to her. You couldn't have her and the SEALs. Are you willing to give up being a SEAL?"

"I made a mistake before, there's no reason I can't have both. She never asked me to choose. That was my mistake, one I plan to make up for now."

"A family deserves more than we can give them." With that, Boom turned on his heels and walked back to his truck.

Ace stood there for a long moment wondering if Boom had a point. Then he shook his head and opened the door. It didn't matter what branch of the military, everyone deserved a chance at happiness and a family, and he wasn't about to miss his opportunity. If he was sure of only one thing, it was that he wouldn't get another chance. There was only now.

Chapter Nine

The seventy-two hours that Ace had on leave flew by in the blink of an eye for Gwen. She'd had all this time with him before he left and now they were down to the last hours. She leaned against the dresser while he added the last remaining items to his duffle bag.

"I can feel you drilling holes into my back." He closed up the bag and turned to her. "It's going to be different this time, I swear. Seven days will go quick and I'll be back here holding you tight. Wynn and Lucky are just a phone call away if you need anything."

"I'll be fine. I've been taking care of myself for years." She forced herself to smile and not think of the last time they were in this predicament.

"I'd never doubt it for a moment. I just want you to know you're not alone." He came to her, slipping his arm around her waist.

"Do you need a ride? Maybe I can make you something to eat before you go?"

"Shh, love." He ran the knuckle of his index finger down her cheek and over her chin. "I'll drive myself and leave my truck on base."

"Food?" She wanted something to do, anything to relieve the unease within her.

"Let's go for a walk."

"Shouldn't you…be leaving?"

"I have time." He slipped his hand into hers. "Come with me, there's a place I want to show you."

"Where are we going?" She let him lead her down the steps and through the house. It wasn't until they were out the back door that she paused. It was the first time she had been out back and nothing had changed. The flagstone patio dominated the back of the house, leading to the pool and hot tub on one side, while the other side was set up for outdoor entertaining. Ace's father designed a perfect outdoor kitchen that fit both his and his wife's needs, allowing for a large grill and plenty of space. Off to the side a flagstone path led down to the creek that backed the property. It was the place where they'd first met.

She balked. "Ace…"

"Every deployment I've gone on, there's one thing I always do before I leave. Do you remember why I go down by the creek?" When she didn't answer, he spoke it aloud as if she had forgotten. "It's where we first met. Your friend Madison lived in the house on the other side of the creek. Wynn, Lucky, and I were down there playing…"

"I remember." She nodded. "It was just after I moved here."

"You, Madison, and Wynn were inseparable after that day." He brought her hand to his lips and placed a gentle kiss on her knuckles. "I've never been able to get you off my mind since."

"It's also where we spent many afternoons before you left." The memories poured forth, bringing back all the good times she had with the whole Diamond family.

"It's the place of many firsts for us. The first time we met, our first kiss, the first time I told you I loved you."

"I don't think we should…" She paused and glanced toward the path again. "It could ruin a spot that means a lot to both of us."

"It won't. I told you I'm coming back to you, not even a herd of wild elephants could keep me away from you. Having you join me on the walk will add another first."

"What do you mean?" She raised an eyebrow in question.

"It will be the first time you've seen me off on military duty. Another first for us and one of many I hope."

She nodded. If she was going to trust things would be different this time, she had to make them different. Ace might have been the one to end things, but he wasn't the only one to blame. She could have tried harder to get in touch with him, to convince him they could make things work. Growing up in a military family, she knew firsthand that military life was tough, and there was no doubt in her mind that SEAL life was harder, but Ace was worth it.

Ace leaned against one of the command vehicles while they waited for Lieutenant Mac García to finish dressing down one of the newest team members, Petty Officer Cannon Bailey. From the look of Cannon when he arrived, he'd been out late partying and overslept. The Lieutenant was already going to ride them hard during training for the scene at the bar the other night, and Cannon's lateness was going to make things worse. Even knowing the next week might resemble *hell week* all over again, Ace didn't care…he could only think about getting back to Gwen.

Damn, that woman had him all turned around with need and desire. Fantasies of getting her naked haunted him day and night. The only thing that had kept it from happening was promising they'd take things slow. After this mission, she'd trust him more and he could get her into his bed.

"How's your instant family?" Boom leaned against the vehicle, watching the other men load the final things onto the plane.

"Don't call Gwen that." Ace glared at Boom and tried to keep from hitting his best friend.

"Man, you left her for a reason. Why are you setting both of you up to get hurt? She deserves better than that."

"I was young and stupid." He was still upset after the last time they had this conversation and didn't want to get into it again with Boom. "I'm not going to screw this up."

"I hope you know what you're doing."

"Just drop it, Boom, this has *nothing* to do with you." Ace's anger was starting to seep into his voice. He was tired of Boom's attitude, and he was sick of the instant family comment. The only thing that stopped him from saying more was García strolling toward them.

Time to get this going…

Chapter Ten

With a deep sigh, Gwen tossed her purse and keys on the table. The first appointment with her new OBGYN had gone well. Her baby girl was healthy and developing right on schedule. In less than five months, she'd have a child to make a life for. So it was now or never for her and Ace to work things out. If he screwed up this time, that was it.

With her feet killing her, she strolled around the living room to the sofa and plopped down. Kicking off her heels, she leaned back against the soft throw pillows and longed for a nap. The flashing from the phone alerting her to a voice mail caught her attention.

Maybe it's Ace. She leaned forward and pressed the glowing red light. Instantly, Ace's voice filled the room.

"I've only got a minute but I remembered you mentioning your appointment was today. Hope everything went great and you can tell me about it soon." Something in the background of the call made Ace pause before continuing. "Don't wait up. It will be late tomorrow when I get back. I miss you."

Just that brief message served to lighten her heart, knowing he was safe. It made her long for him to be with her, to have him share in the moment of her pregnancy, even though it wasn't his child. Finally, she understood how her mother felt anytime there was word from her father, even if it was only a message or a letter. Her dad had missed so many important moments in her life, including most of her parents' anniversaries, and still their family stayed strong, even though the times were tough. Her mom always said military families were made stronger, or else they wouldn't get through it.

The front door creaked open behind her. With no doubt in her mind who it was, she didn't bother to turn around.

"Gwen, you back?" Wynn called out, stepping into the foyer.

"In here."

Wynn sauntered in as if she was hot off a catwalk, always so put together and ready to take on the world. Owning a fashionable boutique—Roll of the Diamond—just off the boardwalk, she had to flaunt her designs. It was perfect for Wynn because she wouldn't be caught dead in jeans and a T-shirt.

How the two of them became inseparable was beyond Gwen. They couldn't have been more different. Where Wynn was a girly girl, Gwen was slightly tomboyish, and preferred her jeans rather than slacks or dresses.

"I brought Pete's Pizza." Wynn sat the box down on the coffee table, and pulled two bottles of water from a bag. "Have you heard from Ace?"

"Today, he'll be home late tomorrow night." Gwen leaned forward and opened the pizza box, revealing the delicious square slices. The squares were thick like pan pizza but crispy and light, and each one could have its own toppings. It was her favorite pizza place and one she'd missed when she moved away.

"Normally he's not able to call much, so it's nice he was able to this time," Wynn said.

"He called the day he left too." She grabbed a slice before leaning back against the sofa, and took a bite. "I know it's not always like this, and there will be times he's gone for a lot longer where I won't hear from him, but it was nice he called."

"I only mentioned it because I want you to understand what you are getting yourself and your daughter into. Is Ace really the man you want?"

"Oh Wynn." Suddenly disgusted by the pizza, she tossed it back into the box.

"Think of me as a friend, not as Ace's sister. Don't get me wrong, it would be amazing to have things work out for you two and to have you as a sister-in-law, but I just want you to know what you're doing. I remember how distraught you were when he cut ties between you two. I don't want to see you go through that again."

"I never stopped loving him. All this time there's never been anyone else, only him."

"You mean…"

"No one." She nodded. "I've dated occasionally but there's never been anyone else I've been intimate with. Why do you think I chose to have a sperm donor? I had no other choice. Other men didn't compare to Ace. They did nothing for me. My heart and body belonged to him."

"You grew up in a military family, are you sure you want that for your daughter?" Wynn perched on the edge of the recliner.

"You didn't grow up with it being engraved into your life like I did. Dad only retired because his health started to decline, otherwise he'd have stayed in until he died. It was his life." She ran her hand over her stomach. "Dad was away a lot and even when he was home he worked crazy hours, but that didn't change how I felt about him. When he was there, he spoiled mom and me, and every moment with him was even more special and cherished."

"You didn't answer me, is that what you want for your daughter?" Wynn pushed.

"I want a life where we're happy. My daughter should grow up surrounded by family and love, where she can become whatever she wants. I'm going to take things one step at a time with Ace, and we'll go from there. If things work out, wonderful…if not, my daughter will have me and I'll have to be enough." She cracked open one of the bottles of water and took a sip. "Ace doing his duty for the country, keeping each of us safe, is an amazing thing. It wouldn't diminish his role in our lives, but would make it stronger. We would cherish the time we have with him. He's a hero."

Wynn smirked. "Don't take me asking as I'm trying to keep the two of you apart. You're my best friend, and like a sister to me, I don't want to see you get hurt again. The last time it caused a riff in the relationship between Ace and me, and we're just getting back to where we were. I don't think it can take another hit like the last time, and I don't want to have to beat the shit out of him again."

"What?"

"Mom and I went to see him for a weekend, it was a couple weeks after you received the letter."

"Tell me you didn't."

Wynn nodded. "I confronted him. Words weren't enough, but when it turned to a fight, it was only my fists flying. He ended up with a black eye and busted lip. It would have been worse but Mom stopped it."

"You shouldn't have done it."

"Why?" Wynn leaned forward, putting her elbows on her knees. "He did wrong by you. A damn letter? Seriously? Mom taught all of us better than that. You should have heard the lecture Dad gave him."

"I never wanted to cause problems in the family." She hated the idea that his family said something to him about what happened. It should have stayed between them, but since she confided in Wynn, it got back to the whole Diamond family. "He did what he thought was best."

"Don't defend his actions, he broke your heart."

"What's more important is he's mending my heart now." Gwen ran her hand down the bottle, wiping away the moisture. She didn't want to think about the past. Right now was a time for new beginnings. In order to do that she had to give up the ghosts of the past.

"What if he breaks it again?"

"Then that's it. I'll pick up the pieces and move on for the sake of my daughter." She set the bottle aside and met Wynn's gaze. "Could we please drop this? The past is what it is. Nothing can change that, but this is a second chance for Ace and me. Couldn't you just be happy for us?"

"I want to be, but I keep thinking about that damn letter."

"I appreciate your concern, but I want to give this a try. I love Ace." As soon as the words left her mouth, she knew it was true. The love for him never ceased or diminished. She loved him and wanted this to work out. They'd make it work.

Chapter Eleven

It was just after two in the morning when Ace pulled into the driveway of his house. Only the light above the door glowed bright through the dark night, welcoming him. For the first time in his career, there was someone waiting for him to come home. Never before did the idea of having someone there appeal to him.

He opened the truck door, thinking of slipping into bed next to Gwen. The notion of feeling her warm body pressed against his hardened his shaft with desire. He reached across the seat and tugged his duffle bag out with him. When he turned around, the front door opened and Gwen stood in the doorway wearing gray yoga pants, a skimpy tank top, and a blanket around her shoulders.

"You didn't have to wait up." Seeing her sent a rush of energy through him. There was a lightness to his steps as he came up the pathway to the house.

"I was in bed when I saw your lights." She stepped out of the way, giving him space to enter. There was an uneasy smile etched on her face, almost like she wasn't sure how to handle the homecoming.

Wanting to ease the tension quickly, he tossed his bag on the floor, kicked the door shut, and went to her. Wrapping his arms around her, he pulled her tight against him. "I've missed you." He almost told her he loved her, but the last thing he wanted was for her to run out the door scared.

"You mean you were gone?" She teased, clinging to him. She ran her hands up his back, as if she was trying to convince herself he was there.

"I know that look in your eye. You missed me." He kissed the top of her head. "Come sit for a moment and tell me how your appointment went. Did you find a house this past week? How much did you miss my arms around you?" He spouted off the questions before she could answer them.

She pulled the blanket tighter around her shoulders and moved to the sofa. "Everything is fine with my pregnancy. My daughter is healthy and growing right on schedule. Though this made me realize I need to figure out a name for her. Other than the appointment, the week was rather quiet. I did see two other places, but the condo next to Lucky's is still my first choice."

"Why not stay here?" He pulled her into his lap and linked his arms around her waist. "I told you this time would be different. Stay with me."

She leaned her head against his shoulder and let out a soft laugh. "My parents would roll over in their graves if they knew I was shacking up with a man before marriage."

"Then marry me."

Her head popped up and her eyes widened. "What?"

"Hear me out." He held tight as she started to pull away from him. "I've done a lot of thinking this past week. If I wouldn't have screwed up, you'd be my wife, and this would be our child."

"But that's not the case." Sorrow coated her words.

"Not yet, but there's no reason it can't be. You deserve so much better, but I realized this is all I can give you. If you allow me, I'll spend the rest of my life proving you didn't make a mistake. Gwen, I love you. You've always had my heart."

Tears glistened in her eyes. "I love you too."

"Then marry me."

"There's more to marriage than just love. I'm pregnant with another man's child."

He placed his hand on the curve of her stomach, feeling the roundness under his fingers. "Let me be a father to her."

"I thought we were taking this slow." She smirked. "This isn't slow."

"Then just think about it. When you're ready, the offer stands. If we marry before you give birth, she can have the Diamond name and no one needs to know otherwise. She'll be my daughter in every way."

"I need to think about this." She laid her hand over his. "I'm not ashamed of using a sperm donor…"

"Gwen, that's not what I meant. I only meant that if you let me, she would be my daughter in every way. She's a part of you, and I'll love her just like I love you." It didn't matter the child wouldn't be his flesh and blood; she would still be his daughter.

"What about your family?"

He raised an eyebrow in confusion. Wynn and Lucky already knew she was pregnant and it wasn't his, but neither of them had said anything about it. He wasn't sure where her worry was coming from.

"What about them?"

"Wynn stopped by yesterday. She mentioned the two of you got into it pretty good a few weeks after I received the letter."

"I remember. I ended up with a black eye. Even Lucky took a few hits when I saw him. But what does that have to do with right now?"

"Your father laid into you about it too."

He nodded. "I'm still missing the connection."

"I caused all these problems because I shared what happened with Wynn. I never expected her to tell everyone. Oh, your family must hate me."

"It was never your fault, only mine. They don't hate you." He wiped the tears from her cheeks. "During that visit where Wynn took her anger out on my face, Mom told me she always expected we'd get married. She wasn't happy with how I went about things, but she believed things would work out in the end. Maybe if I would have come home sooner, it would have worked out long before now."

"What matters is now."

"Then let's just enjoy that I'm home and you're by my side."

"What did you have in mind?" Her glossy pink lips curled up into a smile.

"Let me take you to bed. I want to hold you close while we sleep. Then in the morning, let's just see what happens then."

"Hmm, morning." She winked at him before slipping off his lap to stand. "I'm tired, so if you're coming…"

"Oh sugar, I'm coming." He took hold of her hand. "I wouldn't miss this for the world."

He didn't care if it took his whole life, he'd convince her he was there for the long haul. Their past was rocky and there were things they'd have to overcome, but they could do it together. The love he had for her was strong enough they could overcome anything. This was the life he was supposed to have years ago and now he was claiming it. He wasn't going to let Gwen slip through his fingers again.

Chapter Twelve

Dressed in a little black cocktail dress that hid the slight curve of Gwen's growing stomach, she fingered the strand of her mother's pearls around her neck, feeling sexier than ever. She checked the mirror again to make sure her hair was spiking in all the right places, before slipping into the heels she had set out. She wanted everything perfect. Going to Wynn's for a small gathering seemed to add more pressure to her relationship with Ace.

Wynn was her best friend, but this one time Gwen wished she'd lay off. She needed time with Ace to work things out. Not to mention time to think about the marriage proposal.

"Gwen?" Ace called from the downstairs landing. "Are you ready yet?"

"Men are always so impatient," she told her daughter, running her hand over her stomach. With one final check, she turned and headed downstairs.

Exiting her room, she found Ace at the top of the stairs. "I heard that."

"You must have hearing like a dog, I barely said it aloud." He stood there with his mouth open, staring at her like he'd never seen her before. "Why are you looking at me like that?"

"Wow." He opened and closed his mouth. "You look beautiful."

"You act like this is the first time ever." Nervous, she bit her lip, waiting for him to stop looking at her like a freak event at a zoo.

"Not the first time, but damn, woman, you blow me away." He closed the distance between them and slipped his arms around her waist. "What do you say about staying in tonight and letting me take you back to bed?"

As tantalizing as that offer sounded, she shook her head. "Tempting, but we made a promise that we'd be at Wynn's tonight."

"Someday my workaholic sister will understand." He leaned his head down into the crest of her shoulder, his warm breath against her skin sending a line of goosebumps down her arm. "Wouldn't you rather stay in and let me cherish your body, make love to you until you scream my name?"

"You've been home two days and now you want me?" She tried to sound hurt but it wasn't working. Every word held a hind of desire rather than disappointment.

"Sweets, I've wanted you, but you wanted to take this slow. It's been incredibly hard but I wanted to do right by you." He kissed her neck, gently dragging his teeth over her skin. "I want you now."

She curled her neck into him, drawing his mouth closer, and a soft moan escaped her lips. Need and desire coursed through her, until she was almost willing to forget the dinner and let him take her. "Ace…"

"Yes?" He kissed along her neck until he reached her earlobe.

"Tonight. After Wynn's. Let's go before my control snaps."

"That's almost an invitation to keep going. Once your control is gone we can forget going out and make it up to Wynn later." He stepped back, and straightened his dress shirt. "Let's get this over with."

"You should be happy to spend the evening with your family."

"She's inviting us to see how things are progressing with us. Wynn has always been the nosiest of all of the Diamond clan." He slipped his hand in hers, and headed for the steps.

"You do realize that is a *major* accomplishment, right?"

He stopped halfway down the steps and raised an eyebrow at her. "Are you saying my family is a bunch of nosy busybodies?"

"Oh, look at the time, we need to be going." She slipped past him, quickly coming down the last steps.

"Gwyneth London." There was a playfulness in his tone as he called after her. "Don't you walk away from me."

"On the risk of repeating myself, we need to be going."

"Answer me, then we can go." He came down the final steps.

"You're not blind, you know what your family is like better than me." She opened the closet door and grabbed their coats. "Lucky and you aren't much better than Wynn."

He took her coat and held out it for her. "I'm going to make you pay for that comment tonight."

"Promises, promises." She handed him his coat and waited while he buttoned the double-breasted jacket.

It was amazing they were able to have such ease between them after what had separated them. If only the ease would continue through the rest of the family. She hadn't told Ace about the conversations she had with Lucky and Wynn urging her to stay away from him because she didn't want to cause any problems between the siblings. Things were going so well now, she could only hope they held their tongues tonight, and didn't bring up what happened when he went off to boot camp.

Ace stood on the balcony, the salty breeze from the ocean beating against him, cooling the desires that ran through him. His last shred of control was hanging by a thin thread, and every ounce of him wanted to rush back inside and whisk Gwen away. In his line of work, he could be called into action any time, and all he could think about was having Gwen naked beneath him before he had to leave again.

The way that short black dress hugged every curve of her body had his shaft hard since she'd stepped out of the bedroom. He never wanted something as much as he wanted her that very moment. Damn Wynn for inviting them. Keeping him here was pure torture.

"We need to talk." Lucky closed the balcony door behind him.

"Then talk." It came out edgier than he meant, but he didn't want to talk, especially not about what Lucky thought they needed privacy for.

"Man, I think you're wrong. Gwen doesn't need this. She doesn't need to have her heart broken again. You weren't around to see what it did to her before, but I was. You either stay with her, or leave her alone. Don't screw with her, she deserves better than that."

"This isn't your business. Stay out of it, Lucky." He clenched the wrought iron banister, refusing to give into his brother's taunts.

"You weren't here before. I was. That makes it my business. Wynn and I helped her put the pieces together. She was a mess, and I don't want to see her go through that again."

Ace spun toward his brother and let the anger flow through him. If Lucky wasn't going to back off, Ace had to make him do it out of self-preservation. "If I didn't know any better, I'd think you had something for her. All those years when she was alone you didn't make your move, but now I'm back and you're jealous. I'll kick your ass if I need to, but this is between Gwen and me."

"You fuck this up and it's going to be about all of us. I won't stand by if I think you're hurting her. Wynn and Dad have my back on this, don't think you'll get off like you did before." Lucky turned back to the door, and grabbed hold of the handle. "Don't mess this up."

"What about Mom?"

"What about her?" Lucky glanced back in question.

"You said Wynn and Dad, but you didn't mention Mom. I heard it all from her before, but you left her out of it."

"Mom is the optimistic one of the family, she thinks this is going to work out and you'll be the first of the Diamond crew to get married." Lucky made it obvious he didn't agree, then opened the door and went back inside, leaving Ace alone on the balcony to consider things.

Married? If only I can convince Gwen…

Chapter Thirteen

Ace was still standing on the balcony, his fingers tight around the banister as he stared off at the endless ocean. The sun had set long ago, leaving darkness in its wake, but with the lights from the condominiums, it was still bright enough to see the waves crash on the beach. The beach was the only appealing thing about Wynn's condo, but he couldn't give up the family home to move and be surrounded by people. When he was home and the SEAL team wasn't there, he needed the quiet; it helped him center himself.

He closed his eyes, taking in the thundering rush of the waves and the draw of the ocean. The sea could be deadly if someone forgot that even for an instant. Reminding him of his job. Would he only end up leaving Gwen as a widow, grieving for him again? Was it fair to her? He cursed himself for letting the doubt creep in again.

"You've been out here a while, is everything okay?"

He opened his eyes to find Gwen standing beside him. "I didn't hear you come out."

She slipped her arm around his waist. "Your forehead is all crinkled together in worry, what's wrong?"

"Nothing." He brought her closer to him and wrapped his arms around her. "How late do we have to stay?"

"You'd think after your last deployment you'd want to spend time with them."

"It's you I want to spend time with." He slid his hand down her hip. "Naked time."

"Then let's go."

"Oh baby." He lowered his head, letting his lips brush softly against hers. "I'm going to make you a very happy woman tonight."

"Are you always so confident?" She teased.

"I'm a SEAL. I've been through *hell week* and survived, so yeah I'm confident. Tonight you'll see I'm not just cocky, but I have what it takes to back it."

With a smirk and a twinkle in her eyes, she stepped back. "Let me say my goodbyes to Wynn and Lucky, and then we can put you to the test."

"You've got five minutes, then I'll carry you out of here if I have to." His body responded as she turned to go back into the house.

Oh yeah, baby, it's time to take all doubt out of her mind.

During the drive across town, Gwen couldn't shake the anger over Wynn's final words. She'd had it with people telling her how to live, thinking they knew best. This was between her and Ace and they'd find their way through all of it if it was meant to be. Otherwise, she'd have to give up on the fantasy of them together and move on with her life. This was their final shot.

All or nothing, Gwen. Give it everything.

"Are you planning to sit here in the car all night? If so I'm sure we could make this work, though I think a bed might be more comfortable."

Ace's voice pulled her from her thoughts, making her realize they had pulled into the driveway. "Sorry." She grabbed the handle and pulled it open.

He laid his hand on her arm before she could slip out of the car. "Second thoughts?"

"No…not at all. I was just thinking about something else, that's all. Now can we go inside? It's chilly." She got out of the car and shut the door before he could say anything else.

Following her lead, he stepped out of the car and met her by the walkway. "Wynn said something to you, didn't she?" When she didn't reply, he added, "I wish they'd just let us live our lives. I hate that she put doubt in your mind."

Anger and sadness crossed his face, pulling at her heart until she reached out and cupped his cheek. "I'm not doubting you."

"I'm going to prove to you…"

"Shh…" She ran her thumb along the line of his jaw, the smooth skin sliding under her fingers like silk. "You've already proven everything to me. Well, except the reason you're so confident."

In answer, he reached down, slid his arm under her legs, and lifted her into his arms. "Let's get this show on the road then."

"Wow, you know I can walk."

"You're a romantic. Don't you want someone to carry you across the threshold?"

She tipped her head back and let out a lighthearted laugh. "That's after a wedding."

"If you'd marry me, I'd carry you over every threshold. For now, this will have to do." He winked at her before strolling toward the house, carrying her with ease.

"We'll talk about it after I see how this confidence of yours plays out." She teased him with a wiggle of her eyebrows.

"So my sexual aptitude will decide our marriage." Still holding her, he managed to unlock the door and step inside. "SEALs have stamina unknown to others. I'll have you screaming my name all night."

"Promises, promises." She teased. Their night together before he shipped off for training was special, but something about the way he acted made her think this was going to blow her world.

He kicked the door shut and swung the lock home. "In a moment, it will be more than just words."

"Let me down."

"Not until you're upstairs and laid out on the bed ready for me." Dashing up the steps two at a time, she used her free hand to work on the buttons of his dress shirt. "Then I'll have my way with you."

In the bedroom, he gently placed her on her feet next to the bed and in one quick move pulled her dress over her head. "Lay back."

"Are you always so demanding?"

"Comes with the territory." He stood there waiting for her to do as he asked, giving her one final chance to back out.

She kicked off her shoes and moved back to the middle of the bed, then leaned back on her elbows waiting for him to join her. "If we're going to be demanding, then you should be just as naked as I am. Out of the dress shirt and jeans."

He tugged the shirt apart, sending the remaining buttons flying. "Is that what you had in mind, sweets?" He unhooked his jeans and let them slide down his hips and onto the floor, until he was standing there in just his boxers with his shaft stretching against the material.

With a shake of her head, she tried to hold back the laughs. "Not entirely, but it works. Now come here."

Without delay, he flopped onto the bed and slid on top of her. "Are you sure about this?"

"Second thoughts?" She started to move up the bed, away from him, and swallowed the fears that were rising within her.

"Not about you, sweets." He pressed his lips to her forehead, sending heat racing through her body.

Laying her hand against his chest, she played with the little patch of hair in the center of his pecs. "I never thought we'd be here…us after all these years, who'd have thought?"

"All that matters is that we are." He reached between her breasts and unhooked her bra. "Now lay back and let me prove I'm worthy to be your husband. Remember that marriage proposal depends on my performance."

She pulled another pillow from the side and shoved it under her head. “I’m waiting.”

Their lips met in a long, slow, deliberate kiss that gave and demanded. He cupped her breasts and teased the nipples, gently swirling his thumbs against the hard buds and then pinching them. Pain mingled with pleasure and her back arched. She forgot about the pressures everyone was putting on them and just enjoyed the moment, feeling what Ace was offering her.

His warm laughter washed over her and he abandoned her mouth, sucking one nipple against his teeth. Sparks of pleasure fired inside her. She hadn’t felt anything like this since that night on the beach. Everything inside her wanted to speed his touch, while another part wanted to enjoy every second as if it could be her last.

He slid his hand under the thin material of her panties and between her thighs, urging them apart. Until his fingers could slide between her folds, finding her special spot, he teased the hard bundle of nerves. His mouth work on one nipple, kissing along the valley between before making his way to the other, all the while his fingers worked to wrench an orgasm from her.

“Ohhh…” She cried out at the climax. The air sizzled around her as he drove her toward the brink again. Opening her eyes, her pleasure soaked gaze found him straddled above her, smirking.

Chapter Fourteen

Gwen threw caution to the wind and slipped her hand down his chest until she could take his shaft in her hand. Wrapping her fingers around him, she slowly slid her hand over his length. With every touch, she embraced the life she wanted. This time she wouldn't give up Ace without a fight.

Her body craved his touch and it had been too long since she felt the gentle caress of another. He pulled his mouth from hers and kissed a path down her neck. Sensations collided and threatened to overwhelm her when he teased her nipples. He slipped on top of her, breaking her hold on him. His bulky frame hovered above her and he stared down at her, desire burning in his eyes.

He caressed every inch of her body, sending moans of ecstasy from her lips. For such a big man, he was incredibly tender, as though trying to memorize every curve of her body with his hands and mouth. Heat soared through her blood and she grew impatient with need, demanding.

"Ace, I want you."

"Not yet." He slipped down her body until he was at her waist. "Soon, first I want to make this memorable. The first of many…"

He blazed a hot, wet trail of kisses across her belly and stroked her thighs with his fingertips. With every touch, she arched her hips, demanding more. She couldn't get enough of him. Nudging her legs farther apart, he cupped her core. His fingers delved inside her and she met the teasing thrusts. A demanding moan she barely recognized vibrated in her throat. Passion drove fire through her, melting the chill in her center. The trail of wicked kisses tingled over her thighs. He moved his hand and replaced it with his mouth. Tiny nips and gentle licks flicked over her sweet spot, nearly driving her over the edge. She grabbed the top of his head, torn between pressing him closer and dragging him up. She wanted all of him.

"Ace, please…" Even in the sexual haze, she realized what she said and those few words changed everything. There was no going back from sex, but in that moment she didn't care, she wanted him inside her.

"All right, sweets." He spread her legs farther before filling her slowly, inch by inch. Halfway in, he slid out before thrusting, filling her completely with his manhood. His strokes fed her fire like tinder set to dynamite.

His hips increased pace, driving the force of each pump. The thrusts became deeper and faster, falling into a perfect rhythm, moving with such precision, as if in a well-choreographed dance. Their bodies rocked back and forth, tension stretching her tighter as she fought for the release she longed for. She dug her nails into his back, arching her body into his when she came. His rhythm stayed strong until he shouted her name as his own climax followed.

He stayed buried deep within her and leaned down to kiss her forehead. "How was that for a performance?"

"Hmm, I think it could be improved." She teased as he slipped out of her and collapsed beside her.

"I'll see if I can improve next round."

"Not just confident, you jump to assumptions."

He slipped his arm around her and pulled her close.

Cuddling tight against Ace, her breath slowly returned to normal, while his fingers caressed her hip in long, lazy strokes. For the first time in a long time, she felt complete. In Ace's arms, she knew she was safe.

"What about the marriage proposal? Did I prove I was worthy of you?"

"You've always been worthy of me." She laid her hand on his chest, teasing along the lines of his abs.

"That doesn't answer my question."

"Ask me properly and you might get an honest answer." She knew the answer she wanted to give, but she wanted it done right.

He smirked at her before pulling his arm from under her head and rolling over. She pulled the sheet over her, hiding her nakedness. "Ace…" Her heart raced. *He couldn't…*

Rolling back over, he held an open ring box. "Gwyneth London, you've had my heart since I found you frolicking down by the creek. you do me the honor of marrying me?"

She leaned forward, forgetting the sheet as it slid down her chest, and giving him her left hand. "Yes."

He slipped a beautiful white gold ring onto her finger, with a large princess diamond in the center, surrounded by smaller diamonds. It was completely stunning.

"Before I left for boot camp I bought this."

"Why?" Tears threatened to fall as she gazed down at the ring. After all these years, it was finally happening. She was going to get her prince charming, or maybe that was supposed to be prince SEAL.

"I thought I'd propose before I left."

"Why didn't you?"

"I went to your father and asked his permission." He propped himself up on his elbow, his fingers laced through hers. "He gave it to me, on the condition that I waited until I returned on my first leave."

"Why?" She felt like she was asking the same thing over and over.

"Your parents' marriage was strong but at the beginning it was rough. Your mother didn't understand what she was getting into when she married a military man."

"But I grew up with it, I knew what I was getting into."

"He just wanted to make sure you understood. SEAL life is harder. I could be called up at any time and have to leave on a deployment. He thought the break while I was training would allow you to realize it completely, therefore giving us a solid foot in our marriage. The first year of marriage is always the hardest, especially for military families. He was trying to do right by his only daughter."

"Then he was the first of the crumbling blocks that ended things with us."

"No." He squeezed her hand. "That was completely my fault."

She leaned back against the pillows and drew the back of her hand down his jawline. "Things worked out in the end."

"That they did." He took his hand from hers and laid it on her stomach. "I'd like to marry before…"

"Why is that important?"

"I want this to be prefect. I want *our* daughter to have the Diamond name."

Our daughter.

Her heart skipped a beat. When he'd arrived a few weeks ago, all she could think to do was run, run before he had a chance to break her heart again. Now there she was in bed with him, accepting his proposal, and talking about their daughter. It was almost more than she could believe. Things were nearly perfect. If only Wynn and Lucky could see what was between them without remembering the past.

Chapter Fifteen

A roaring fire spread heat through the living room, keeping Gwen cozy as she dozed on the sofa while waiting for Ace to return from the base. Three weeks had passed since she had accepted his proposal, yet they were still keeping it from the rest of the Diamond gang. Wynn's reaction when she found out was going to be the worst of any of them. It was destined to be a disaster.

"Your Auntie Wynn will come around, don't you worry." She rubbed her stomach, trying to calm her daughter. The somersaults were beginning to make her queasy.

Wynn was stubborn and getting her to come around could take time. Lucky would be supportive, but cautious; he was already like a brother to her. The Diamond parents were another story, the unknown factor in the equation. "It's going to be okay." She whispered to herself, trying to calm her nerves.

The front door opened, sending a rush of cold air through the house. "Sweets, I'm home."

"In here." She scooted up on the sofa and tucked her legs under her. "How was work?"

"Same old, same old. Mom called, they're an hour away and very excited to see you again." He'd barely sat in the chair cattycorner from the sofa when he shot up and came to her. "Sweets, are you okay?"

She swallowed the lump in her throat but couldn't quite calm herself.

"You've turned green. You're not worried about Mom?"

"Me, worried?" She tried to make light of it, but her stomach churned.

"Everything is going to be fine. Mom always said we would work things out, and now we have." He cupped her hands. "She's going to be excited this happened, and she's going to be a grandmother. Anyway, it doesn't matter what anyone thinks, only that we're happy. Are you happy with the decision?"

"Yes…but what about Wynn?"

"Wynn is going to be fine. She'll come around, don't worry."

"Having the family gathered together to tell them all at once seemed a good idea when you set it up, but now it's so much pressure. What if things go awful? It could be a disaster."

"Then we ask them to leave. This isn't about them, it's our happiness that matters." He ran his thumb over her knuckles. "Stop worrying."

"Maybe you could take my mind off it." She licked her lips and wiggled her eyebrows. Having him naked again would keep her mind off the stress.

"Unless you want to make the announcement at a restaurant I should get dinner on."

"I'll help." She started to slide her legs off the sofa before he stopped her.

"Rest. I know you're tired, I'll get things started then I need to shower and change."

"I wouldn't be tired if you didn't keep me up all night." She paused, unable to stifle a yawn. "How you don't have circles under your eyes I don't know."

"The need for sleep was kicked out of me long ago." He leaned in and kissed her. "Everything is going to be fine, I promise."

When he headed to the kitchen, she let her head rest against the cushion of the sofa for a moment, and tried to gather her nerves. Being with Ace was what she wanted, what did she care if Wynn or the others weren't happy? What mattered was he made her happy. He was the man she had given her heart to years ago, and in a few months he would be her husband and a father to the child she carried. Things couldn't have worked out better if she had planned it.

Standing on the back deck, Ace cracked open a beer bottle, watching the fall leaves scatter through the air.

Instead of giving him a second of peace, Lucky followed him. He rolled his shoulders and was ready to have it out with his brother. "Just get it out, so we can put this tension behind us. Though keep in mind, nothing you say is going to change it. So you might want to keep your mouth shut, and then I won't have to whoop your ass." He spun on his heels but instead of finding Lucky as he suspected, their father, Buck, stood there.

"Boy, I know you haven't lost your mind enough to speak to me that way." Even as a grown man, Buck's voice still managed to make him backtrack.

"Dad! I meant it for Lucky. I've already heard his input on my interest with Gwen, I thought he had returned for a second round."

"Lucky can wait. It's time you hear from me. I wasn't pleased with how you ended things with Gwen before."

"I know, but this time is different. I screwed up."

"Damn right you did, and you broke your mother's heart in the process. Not to mention the state you left Gwen and the whole damn family."

"Dad…"

"I don't want to hear any excuses. I just want you to know if you screw this up again, you're going to have all of us wanting a piece of your ass. Gwen is a good girl; she deserves better than what you've done to her in the past. I'm damn surprised she didn't move on and find herself a good husband, someone who could treat her right." He glared at Ace, everything about the look reminding him just how angry his father was before. "You're not just getting a wife, but a child. You screw this up and you can find yourself a new family. Your mother and I raised you right, I won't have you disgracing the Diamond name." With that, Buck turned and walked back into the house.

"Well, that could have gone better." Ace leaned against the railing.

"What did you think would happen?" Lucky stepped out of the house, taking a swig from his beer. "We were all left to put the pieces together while you were across the country living it up. Gwen could barely walk into the house without tears springing to her eyes."

"I know I fucked up before." With a clunk, he set his beer on the railing. "I failed her and the whole family, but not this time."

"For her sake, I hope not." Lucky leaned against the railing, as cool as the air that whipped around them. "That's not why I came out here. I came to congratulate you."

"What?" He wasn't sure if he heard his brother correctly.

"Congratulations on getting your act together. Marrying Gwen might be the first thing you've done without your head up your ass and in your career. She's always loved you and now she's going to make an honest man out of you. I wish you both all the best." Lucky stepped away from the railing and headed for the door. "Don't screw this up."

Ace stood there alone with anger pulsing through him. He was tired of people thinking he was going to break Gwen's heart again. Did his family think so little of him? Sure, he had made his fair share of mistakes in the past, but he wasn't that bad a person.

He had just polished off the last of his beer when Gwen opened the door. "I thought you were going to stick by my side tonight. Instead, I get trapped in the kitchen with Wynn. Your mom came to my rescue."

"Come here." He placed the empty beer bottle on the railing and held out his hand to her. She crossed the patio quickly. He wrapped his arms around her and pulled her against his chest. "I'm sorry for leaving you alone with Wynn, I just needed a breather. My family can be a bit intense."

"You're telling me."

"Do I need to have a talk with my baby sister?" He ran his hands down her back, enjoying the feel of her pressed against him.

"It's fine, she's just concerned. Your mom already had a few choice words for her. How did things go with Lucky and your dad?"

"Could have gone worse. Lucky congratulated me on getting my head out of my ass."

"Who'd have thought your mom would be the most supportive." She chuckled, sending the vibrations through him.

"I know you're upset Wynn isn't supportive too, but she'll come around. She's just worried her asshole brother is going to break your heart again."

"You won't," she whispered.

He kissed the top of her head. "I love you."

The love he had for her was stronger than anything he ever felt before. He wasn't about to mess it up.

"Look…" She pointed to the edge of the lawn. The moonlight was coming through the trees, casting a white, heart-shaped glow. "It's an omen."

"An omen of our love…It'll last through the darkest times and go on forever."

He lowered his head and claimed her lips.

Marissa Dobson

Born and raised in the Pittsburgh, Pennsylvania area, Marissa Dobson now resides about an hour from Washington, D.C. She's a lady who likes to keep busy, and is always busy doing something. With two different college degrees, she believes you are never done learning.

Being the first daughter to an avid reader, this gave her the advantage of learning to read at a young age. Since learning to read she has always had her nose in a book. It wasn't until she was a teenager that she started writing down the stories she came up with.

Marissa is blessed with a wonderful supportive husband, Thomas. He's her other half and allows her to stay home and pursue her writing. He puts up with all her quirks and listens to her brainstorm in the middle of the night.

Her writing buddy Pup Cameron, a cocker spaniel, is always around to listen to her bounce ideas off him. He might not be able to answer, but they're helpful in their own ways.

She loves to hear from readers so send her an email at marissa@marissadobson.com or visit her online at http://www.marissadobson.com.

Other Books by Marissa Dobson

Alaskan Tigers:

Tiger Time

The Tiger's Heart

Tigress for Two

Night with a Tiger

Trusting a Tiger

Alaskan Tigers Box Set Volume One

Jinx's Mate

Two for Protection

Bearing Secrets

Tiger Tracks

Healing the Clan

Alaskan Tigers Box Set Volume Two

Her Black Tiger

Forever Creek Shifters:

Forever Fight

Crimson Hollow:

Romancing the Fox

Loving the Bears

A Lion's Chance

Swift Move

Stormkin:

Storm Queen

Reaper:

A Touch of Death

SEALed for You:

Ace in the Hole

Explosive Passion

Operation Family

Marine for You:

Lucky Chance

Back from Hell

A Marines Second Chance *Crossover to the SEALed for You series

Beyond Monogamy:

Theirs to Treasure

Cedar Grove Medical:

Hope's Toy Chest

Destiny's Wish

Leena's Dream

Fate:

Snowy Fate

Sarah's Fate

Mason's Fate

As Fate Would Have It

Half Moon Harbor Resort:

Learning to Live

Learning What Love Is

Her Cowboy's Heart

Half Moon Harbor Resort Volume One

Clearwater:

Winterbloom

Unexpected Forever

Losing to Win

Christmas Countdown

The Surrogate

Clearwater Romance Volume One

Small Town Doctor

Stand Alone:

SEALed Rescue

SEALed in Texas

Starting Over

Secret Valentine

Restoring Love

www.ingramcontent.com/pod-product-compliance
Lightning Source LLC
Chambersburg PA
CBHW020619130626
46552CB00003B/1042

* 9 7 8 1 9 3 9 9 7 8 9 0 5 *